John Todhunter

Forest Songs, and Other Poems

John Todhunter

Forest Songs, and Other Poems

ISBN/EAN: 9783744714730

Printed in Europe, USA, Canada, Australia, Japan

Cover: Foto ©Andreas Hilbeck / pixelio.de

More available books at **www.hansebooks.com**

AND OTHER

TODHUNTER

5/-

Jas. Aurigitmau

FOREST SONGS

AND OTHER POEMS

FOREST SONGS

AND OTHER POEMS

BY

JOHN TODHUNTER

AUTHOR OF

" LAURELLA, AND OTHER POEMS," "ALCESTIS," "A STUDY OF SHELLEY,"
" THE TRUE TRAGEDY OF RIENZI," ETC.

LONDON

KEGAN PAUL, TRENCH & CO., 1, PATERNOSTER SQUARE

1881

TO

D. L. T.

CONTENTS.

―◦―

FOREST SONGS.

SONG-TIDE.

CONTENTS.

SONNETS.

FOREST SONGS.

ERRATA.

Page 15, *after*

  " His entrails I tore with my raging beak '

  Insert

THE THREE BIRDS.

Judas, Judas ! thy cursed deed
Has made the five wounds of Christ to bleed !

Page 99, *for*

  " When Life and Love, the twins were torn apart "

  Read

  Where Life and Love, etc.

B

PRELUDE.

FROM corn bread, and wine from the sunned grape-
clusters ;
From the balm of the Forest these songs.

A SONG OF DAWN.

1.

I CALLED grey Night to speak my doom,
    Wandering in tears,
Peopling the wilderness of gloom
    With shadowy fears.

2.

I met glad Morn upon the hills
    Walking in light,
And all that cloud of threatening ills
    Fled at her sight.

A SONG IN SADNESS.

1.

WHAT ails my heart? 'Twere all in vain
I strove to sound its tide of pain.
What bodes this gloom, this vague distress,
This dreariness, this dreariness?

2.

The wind that wails through yonder pine
Wails lonelier through this heart of mine;
Yet whence this brooding cloud of woe
I cannot tell, I do not know.

3.

Is't vanished love—remorse—or hate
Of life, that leaves me desolate?
Or hope grown sick? Or age that brings
Sad memories of belovèd things?

4.

The rain that drips from yonder bough
With wintrier boding chills my brow ;
Yet why, alas ! it should be so
I cannot tell, I do not know.

THE LOST CHILD.

1.

A CRY is on the mountains wild—
It is the cry of a lost child;
Like a lost lamb's its bleating cry,
"O mammy, mammy!" to the sky:
And the sky, with azure smile,
Never answers it the while.

2.

The mother stares from field to field—
Where can her Hans'l lie concealed?
From mother's wrath to mother's fear
She flies, but finds him far nor near.
To all the Saints she cries in vain,
Then to the Spirits makes her plain.

3.

" Thou Wassermännli, what have I done
That thou shouldst take my little son?
Upon the stone beside the lake,
I never failed to leave thy cake."
And to the water wails she wild:
"Give back my child! give back my child!"

4.

The child forlorn went crying still
Up the hill and down the hill,
Till a Cross he came upon,
Where, 'twixt the Virgin and St. John,
The Blessed Saviour bled and wept—
There he laid him down and slept.

5.

The weary mother found the place:
He slept with tear-beblubbered face.
She clutched her Hans'l, boxed his ears,
And then she kissed away his tears.
Thou Blessed Mother, when we stray,
Do thou the same for us, we pray!

THE GREY MAN.

I.

A WILD wind shakes the sashes,
  The Forester sits alone,
And cold his heart as the ashes
  Upon his cold hearth-stone.

2.

The table stands in the middle,
  Uncleared of the morning meal,
And the unspun flax hangs idle
  From the silent spinning-wheel.

3.

The clock with its dreary ticking
  Makes loneness more forlorn,
And hark ! how caught its cuckoo
  That dismal note since morn ?

4.

And the wind comes whishing and sighing
    By fits in the Witch's Oak,
And over the rooftree flying
    Hoarsely the ravens croak.

5.

A gleam of sunset glistens
    Blood-red on the sanded floor;
The Forester starts and listens—
    What hand taps at the door?

6.

Oh, comes she, reproachless, eager
    To lay with one loving kiss
The guilty ghosts that beleaguer
    His soul with a dread like this?

7.

Mayhap some ten-miles-off neighbour
    With news she has passed his way?
"In God's name, enter!"—There enters
    A lean old man in grey.

8.

What means this mopping and mowing?
  The Forester's heart turns sick,
As hobbling, grinning, and bowing,
  He enters—he and his Stick!

9.

What devil's work is beginning?
  What shrieks by the Witch's Tree,
As hobbling, bowing, and grinning,
  He enters—his Stick and he?

10.

His nerveless arm grips tightly
  That lean old man in grey,
And over the threshold lightly
  They hurry away, away!

11.

Over the threshold leaping
  That goblin Stick goes first,
And next goes the Grey Man, keeping
  Ever his gripe accurst.

The Forester's feet seem flying,
   The Grey Man hobbles so fast,
And round them, shrieking and sighing,
   The forest bends to the blast.

13.

Fast, faster! To work they buckle
   In earnest; the pace grows dire—
With many a gleeful chuckle
   The Grey Man skips through the mire.

14.

Whither, oh whither speed they?
   What end to this dreadful race?
These paths, where no Christ hangs, lead they
   To yonder unhallowed place?

15.

The Forest's most lone recesses
   O'ergloom the Unfathomed Pool;
'Tis fishless, and bud ne'er blesses
   Its margin from Yule to Yule;

16.

Its deadly ways are a wonder—
  Like stone sinks raft or boat,
Drawn down, sucked noiselessly under;
  But sound it, and lead will float.

17.

O God ! as the moon smiles drearly,
  He suddenly sees it—there,
Like the eye of the murdered, blearly
  Its waters accursed glare !

18.

Their wild race ends by the margent,
  The Stick hath wrought its charm,
And, sneering, that grisly sergeant
  Releases his prisoner's arm.

19.

"All hail ! In this devil's cottage
  Your good wife lies at rest,
Your cheer shall be Esau's pottage,
  Your pillow her clay-cold breast."

20.

A shriek of unearthly laughter,
  Re-echoed in thunders dread,
And, Stick first and Grey Man after,
  They've splashed in, heels over head !

21.

Sudden the tempest ceases
  When sunk are the goblin pair,
And herding her silver fleeces
  The moon shines wondrous fair.

22.

Alone with the awful brilliance,
  In silence that takes the breath,
He stands—from man's kindly millions
  Remote as a soul in death.

23.

But hark ! what a gruesome twitter
  Begins from yon blasted pine !
What eyes of accusers glitter
  Like ghosts' in the pale moonshine ?

24.

There, cuddled like traitor cravens,
  Sit gibbering three fiendlike fowls—
You could not say they were ravens,
  You could not say they were owls.

25.

It thrills to his inmost marrow,
  The song of those baleful birds;
Each note, like a poisoned arrow,
  Sows seed of venomous words.

THE FIRST BIRD.

I fretted Pilate over the sea,
He drowned himself to be rid of me;
And when he lay weltering on the beach
I picked his red hands and left them to bleach.

THE THREE BIRDS.

Pilate! Pilate! leap in the flood,
And wash thy hands of that woman's blood!

THE SECOND BIRD.

I sat on the back of Caiaphas' chair,
I whispered sin, and I sang despair,
And when he lay strangled upon his bed,
I tore the tongue from his crafty head.

THE THREE BIRDS.

Thou Caiaphas! where is thy loving wife?
Thy tongue's false witness hath reft her life!

THE THIRD BIRD.

I roosted near when Judas was born,
I sang in his ear till he hung on the thorn,
And when he had fall'n with a ghastly shriek
His entrails I tore with my raging beak.

x   See Errata.

THE FIRST BIRD.

In!

THE SECOND BIRD.

In!

THE THIRD BIRD.

In!

THE THREE BIRDS.

Or we follow thee, follow thee;
Till thou wert happy that Hell should swallow thee!

26.

He hears, and with fixed eyes staring,
    As drawn by a snakish spell,
He glares at the water, glaring
    Snake-still as the eye of Hell.

27.

The Birds are after him—quaking
    He draws to the fatal verge,
Great blood-gouts the surface breaking,
    The fathomless deeps upsurge ;

28.

The Birds are after him—stooping
    Upon him with claws and beak—
He feels the wind of their swooping,
    He hears their appalling shriek.

29.

They shriek, they gibber, they twitter,
    They darken the moon's pale beam,
Till into the caldron bitter
    He leaps, with a shuddering scream.

FOREST-POOL.

I.

Is there a thing more sweet
Than thus to sit——my feet
Deep in this forest-pool,
So clear, and ah ! so cool,
    Hid from the sun-sick noon?

c

ON THE SEUFZERS-BANK.

I.

WHERE is thy breast, bright Daughter of the Morn?
  Where are thine arms to give my longing rest,
That I may die, and find myself new-born?
        Where is thy breast?

2.

Oh, let thy beauty pasture my desire,
  Appease, arouse, sustain me in some sphere
Where passion's tears may turn to action's fire!
        Appear! appear!

LONELY FLOWERS.

I.

LONELY in the light of morning,
In the Forest's gladed stillness,
Exiled from the flowery meadows,
Trembling stand three delicate hairbells.

2.

Pale, forsaken of your kindred,
Wherefore, like estrays of azure
Lured by forest-pools from heaven,
Lurk ye here, ye tremulous hairbells?

3.

In the footsteps of the morning,
Lonely wandering in the wildwood,
I alone have seen the vision
Of your solitary beauty;

4.

And I know not why ye haunt me
Like familiar things, yet strangely,
With dim, ghostlike sense of strangeness,
Mystify this shadowy woodland.

5.

In the footsteps of the morning,
Through forgotten fields of dreamland
Wandering, have my lonely footsteps
Stirred, long since, this virgin stillness?

6.

Do these dew-dimmed branches know me?
Or these crags and shadowy places?
What embalmed enchantment breathe I,
That enraptures and affrights me?

7.

Witchlike, sphynxlike, dumb for ever,
Hang their heads, those desolate hairbells;
Some mysterious past concealing,
Some mysterious fate foreboding,

WATERFALL.

I.

I HEARD a brook, new-weanèd from a cloud,
  Sing in a glen, as down the rocks it sprang :
It clapt its watery hands, and laughed aloud,
    And silver-voiced it sang :—

2.

"Throw off thy swaddling clothes, thou child
    grown grey,
  Leap, like a naked babe, into the sun ;
Hive, beelike, joy on joy the livelong day
    Till thy soul's cells o'errun.

3.

"Joy is the golden honey of the wise,
  The nectar of the strong.   O fool forlorn,
From all the fulness that about thee lies
    Suck joy, and be new-born !"

A SYMPOSIUM.

I.

OVER the mountains, over the meadows
    Dreamily roaming,
Caught by the twilight, I strayed in the Forest
    Self-outlawed, alone.

2.

Deeper the shade grew, deeper the silence;
    Only the spruces,
Gathering around me, frowning above me,
    Gloomily whispered.

3.

Only, at times, the far voice of the valley
    Stirred, through the loneness,
Memories of man and his world in my spirit,
    Remote as a ghost.

Something exultant, something audacious
    Surged in my soul then :
" I am your comrade, ye forests, ye mountains !"
    Proudly I sang.

5.

Softly the moon grew bright in the heavens ;
    Mounted serenely,
Ambushed she shone, till over the pine-tops
    She looked in my face.

6.

And I was mute—my song ceased ; the vast silence,
    Ebbed for a moment,
Flowing, o'erwhelmed me ; then—was it thunder
    That scornfully laughed ?

7.

Then was I 'ware of a Giant beside me,
    Tall as a pine-tree,
Towering above me, laughing like thunder,
    Scornfully laughing—

8.

. Tall as two pine-trees, gloomily laughing !
       Out of the twilight
Gleamed his great face, hale and red as a Viking's
       Bearded with eld.

9.

Cloud-grey his hood was, spruce-green were his gar-
       ments,
       Lordly his presence ;
Frostily keen as the stars of mid-winter
       Flashed his fierce eyes—

10.

Fierce, yet a twinkle of savage good-humour
       Bade me take courage.
Boldly I greeted him : "Wotan the wanderer,
       Why dost thou laugh ? "

11.

Wordlike the thunder pealed down from his summit :
       "Thou art our comrade,
Inch of an earth-worm ! Call'st thou me Wotan ?
       Spruce is my name.

12.

" I am the hoary life of this Forest ;
   I am the spirit
Breathing whose breath, in winterless greenness
   Wax mighty these hosts."

13.

Crestfallen I stood. In savage good-humour,
   Down sat the Giant,
Whistled a gnome from a cave in the forest :
   " Pipes, lad, and beer ! "

14.

Lo, a new wonder ! Back in a twinkling
   Came the swart Kobold,
Bringing two stone-ware mighty-mouthed flagons
   Brimmed with spruce-beer ;

15.

Bringing two pipes with stems like huge branches,
   Which, in a twinkling,
Deftly he filled with balm of the pine-wood,
   Lit with a glow-worm.

16.

Towering above me rose a tall flagon,
    Stretching beside me
Lay a huge pipe-stem. "Ho! ho!" laughed the Giant:
    "Comrade, your health!"

17.

Wistfully up the sides of my flagon,
    Cliff-like above me,
Looked I bewildered. Lo! from a fissure
    Gurgled a beer-fall!

18.

Gurgled a beer-fall, foaming and sparkling
    Down to the valley.
Gravely I pledged him, out of my hat-brim:
    "Comrade, to you!"

19.

Then from my pipe its exquisite odour
    Blandly imbibing,
Cross-legged in front of its mouth-piece, I asked him:
    "What think you of man?"

20.

Verily, as though some jest had broke covert—
 Luring slow laughter
Through his mind's maze to stolidly course it
 Half the night long,—

21.

Holding at poise his flagon uplifted,
 Blankly my Giant
Stared a long stare, then suddenly thundered
 Into huge mirth.

22.

" Man ! Think of man ?—that mischievous vermin !
 Man ? By Thor's hammer,
Earth when she spawned so filthy a creature
 Must have been mad !

23.

" All things were good till, crawling and climbing,
 Rooting and tearing,
Out brake this pest, this itch of creation,
 Scabbing Earth's face.

" Then, when meek Earth, with Brahmin-like patience,
      Bore with his tickling,
Spared him her nails, save one or two scratches,
      Hoped he would mend ;

25.

" Bolder he grew, and fuller of malice,
      Fuller of mischief ;
Over the world, he spread like a tetter,
      Ugliest of things ;

26.

" Blasted his betters, fought with his fellows,
      Planted diseases ;
Till the World-Spirit, in shame and in loathing,
      Vowed he should die :—

27.

" Vowed he should die ; but scorning his slaughter
      Left him to slowly
Seethe in his own most virulent venom—
      Left him to think ;

28.

" Left him to learn his shame, and despairing
    Worship despair, till
Orgy on hopeless orgy consumes him
    Out of the world."

29.

Thus having said, he lapsed into silence,
    Scornfully smoking ;
While his uncultured views of man's nature
    I gently assailed ;

30.

Filled his great ears with great words—Evolution,
    Progress, Art, Culture ;
Steeped him in science, statistics, æsthetics,
    In sweetness and light ;

31.

Gleaned the best books of all the best authors—
    Quoted him Darwin,
Quoted him Spencer, Huxley, and Wallace,
    Talked prose and talked verse ;

32.

Talked till he dozed, overcome—till his snoring
 Sounded no longer,
Talked till, behold, day dawned, and my Giant—
 No Giant was there !

33.

Then I arose, and down through the Forest
 Walked in the dawnlight,
Solemnly, slowly, through the grey spruces,
 Dimmed with sweet dew ;

34.

Down through the dew-drenched glades, through the
 meadows,
 Down to my Gasthof;
Wondering what God could say for man's nature
 And place in the world.

BIRDS OF PREY.

„Kinder zeugen, und die nähren so gut es vermag."

I.

Two Ravens sat upon an oak,
  Two Hawks upon a pine,
And thus they spoke, with scream and croak,
  When the day began to shine.

2.

The Hawks said : " Deep in a forest brake
  There lies a wounded roe,
What will ye give us that ye make
  Your profit of his woe ? "

3.

The Ravens answered : " By yonder wood
  Two wheatears have their nest,
To-day come fluttering forth their brood,
  And ye may choose the best."

4.

The Hawks flew north, and the Ravens south,
 With many a scream of glee,
For the Ravens' nestlings cried from a crag,
 The Hawks' from a tall pine-tree.

5.

The Ravens pecked out the roe's two eyes,
 While still he drew his breath,
He shuddered, and with piteous cries
 Went blindly to his death.

6.

The Hawks pounced down on the wheatears
   brood,
 And bore the best away;
The wheatears shrieked through their happy wood
 For terror and woe that day.

7.

The sun shone gay that livelong day,
 Nor heeded each plaintive shriek,—
The sun were mad if he looked sad
 When the strong oppress the weak.

SLEEPLESS.

I.

I ASKED the woods, and I asked the streams
To send me quiet, and happy dreams.

2.

But Night was angry, and sent instead
Her ugliest goblins to vex my bed.

3.

'Twas not my sorrows, nor vain love-thirst :
My half-starved sins, 'twas, that plagued the worst.

D

EVENING SONG.

1.

THE winds are lulled, the rain-clouds break,
    The cow-bells tinkle near and far,
Calm is the Lake, and o'er the Lake
      One star.

2.

Sweet is the hour when friends apart
    Draw close through eve's tranquillity;
Sweet is the hour, and all my heart
      With thee.

THE HAZEL.

I.

THERE at last the lightning flashes,
   And the hail will soon come down,
And too close the thunder crashes,
   And we have not reached the town.

2.

Come, my child, beneath this hazel
   Couch beside me on the moss ;
For the lightning shuns the hazel
   As the Devil shuns the cross.

3.

Once the Blessed Mary wandered
   With the Saviour in her arms,
And the Devil, for spite, against her
   Raised a tempest by his charms.

4.

Then she knelt beside a hazel,
  And she prayed to God most high;
And the lightning feared to harm her,
  And the Devil was forced to fly.

LONGING.

1.

WHEN the sun flamed fiercely on me
  Longed I for the rain,
When the rain beat cold upon me,
  For the sun again.

2.

All our life is but a longing,
  Joy's but one sweet sigh,
All our life is but a longing,
  Cease to long, we die.

FOLKSONG AT SUNSET.

1.

Down the west, in saffron splendour,
Walks the Day; his vast effulgence,
Flooding all the western pine-woods,
Through their gloom makes aisles of glory.

2.

Far above me, westward gazing,
Mightier than crag-grasping eagles,
Huge, like titans of the sunset
Glow three veterans of the Forest;

3.

And below me, from the valley
Float faint, thrilling wafts of music,
Voices lilting loud some folksong—
Maidens' voices—shrill, sweet voices:

4.

Some rude tale of peasant lovers,
In forgotten graves immortal
In the birdlike songs of peasants,
Lilted loud by peasant maidens.

5.

On the wandering wind of sunset,
Hale with forest balm, that folksong,
Like the wind's mysterious spirit
Floating, floods my heart with longing.

BY THE SCHLUCHSEE.

1.

GREY twilight out of the Forest
  Comes flying on downy wings,
The bats fly forth to meet her
  With petulant twitterings.

2.

The gathering dews are bending
  The long grass drowsily,
In meadows left by the mower
  This night for the moths and me.

3.

The beautiful moths come hovering
  Like restless ghosts in white,
The fond white moths fly trooping
  To burn at my bed-room light.

4.

Soft night sinks down on the Forest,
  I sink on my Gasthof bed,
And sigh for some splendid candle
  To burn my wings at instead.

FOREST MYSTERY.

I.

DEEP within the haunted Forest
Lies a plot of gladed stillness,
Secret as a maiden's longing,
Sweet as lovers' vows new-whispered.

Rarely mortal foot can find it,
Rarely mortal eye behold it;
None can tell if Autumn bleaken,
Winter waste, or Spring restore it.

Only when with sunny tresses
Blue-eyed June flies through the Forest,
Breathing love, its ominous vision
Scares the solitary hunter.

Woe betide the happy lover
Who with fated foot shall find it !
Woe betide the ill-starred lover
Whose o'erhardy eye behold it !

II.

Lovelier glade wind ne'er o'er-wandered,
And the sunbeams and the moonbeams,
Through the woodbine and wild-roses
Glimmering, make all sweet things sweeter;

But from rank, rich lilacs, blooming
All forlorn in that wild Forest,
Wafts of heavy perfume floating
Fill the soul with bodeful dreaming ;

And the wind comes whispering, sighing,
Through dim cypresses that strangely
Haunt the woods with alien presence,
Gloomily gazing till you shudder ;

And, deep-hid in tangled roses,
Lurks a nightingale, and warbles
All day long and all night long there
Songs of yearning and foreboding.

For the blood of murdered lovers
At the root lies of the lilacs,
And the cypresses are waving
O'er the grave of murdered lovers.

III.

O ye cypresses and lilacs,
Mysteries of the lonely wild-wood,
I, the solitary hunter,
Come with fated feet to find you !

Tell me, with the wind conspiring,
What dread thing of me ye whisper?
What dares yet my fate more bitter?
What new woe can ye foretell me?

O thou nightingale that singest
All day long and all night long there,
I, the ill-starred happy lover,
I alone have found thy covert !

Tell me what sad song thou singest?
Wherefore should thy warbling chill me
With its yearning and foreboding,—
With its yearning—its foreboding?

SONG.

1.

BRING from the craggy haunts of birch and pine,
     Thou wild wind, bring
Keen forest odours from that realm of thine,
     Upon thy wing !

2.

O wind, O mighty, melancholy wind,
     Blow through me, blow !
Thou blowest forgotten things into my mind,
     From long ago.

SWALLOW FLIGHT.

I.

Yes, once more ; for, like the swallow
Holding in her heart the vision
Of her nesting-nook last summer,
Back I fly to thee, my Forest !

2.

So farewell to Freiburg minster,
Where the angels of the sunshine,
Gliding in through glowing windows,
On their plumes bring peace from heaven.

3.

Where the sunset-angels freely,
Through the spire of airy fretwork
Wing their way, and, for mere love's sake,
Kiss the cowering gargoyle-demons.

4.

Not the Himmelreich detains us,
With its slopes of orchard-meadow,
Not the Höllenthal beguiles us,
With its crags and misty pinewoods.

5.

Past the meadow and the pinewood,
Lumbering in the dull Post-Wagen,
Little boots it that our thought flies
With the swiftness of the swallow;

6.

Lumbering on, or glad to leave them,
Changing horses, beer imbibing,
While we breathe the balmy freshness,
And trudge onward, rain defying.

7.

Till at last we leave behind us
Mist, and rain, and dull Post-Wagen,
And we seek the friendly Gasthof,
Timbered from its native pinewood.

8.

There my Forest darkly stretches
Over dale and over mountain ;
There my Titi-See lies sparkling,
Shimmering back the sunlit spruces.

EVENING PRIMROSE.

SWEET as a dream of one beloved, yon star,
Sole in the skies, the placid Evening Star
Floats glimmering o'er the sunset-lighted pines
Upon the mountain's brow, and trembling drinks
The ether cool, and blends its trembling ray
With evening's colours in the stream.   I hear
The vale's serenest voice, in murmurs low
From rivulets dim, and in the rippling tune
Of cowbells, as the gathering herds flow down
From upland pastures home—a gurgling brook
Of cool and silver sound.   The wild, sad, sweet
Accords that chime at fitful intervals,
As wills it wanton chance, wake in my heart's
Most lonely cave its melancholy spring,
Whose waters, trembling into gloomy peace,
Image delights more deep than ever grew
By mortal mere, or brook the eager hands
Of passionate desire.
                    But now the voice

Of the glad vale, the vision of its peace,
Fade from my brooding sense—grow but a vague
And distant dream ; such alien forms arise,
Born of my reading of to-day, between ;
And baleful as a murderer's sudden torch,
Scaring the moon upon a night of joy,
And making love-dilated eyes to shrink,
Another scene grows vivid to my view.   .

    The star of love has vanished in the glare
Of Eastern noon ; the golden pine-woods fade
In sun-baked steppes and bleak Tartarian hills ;
For thronging cows, the kneeling camels clank
A few harsh bells ; and for the valley's voice
Are heard wild shouts, and laughter, and the din
Of a victorious host.   The conquerors feast
In silken luxury in a royal tent,
While on their mirth a gory head looks down
From a spear planted in the doorway.   That
Is the defeated Khan's head.   All around
Fierce Turcomans divide the spoil of war—
Horses and camels, victuals, raiment, arms,
And bleeding captives.   On a basking rock,
A bowshot off, stray vultures, come too late
To gorge their fill of slaughter, one by one

Light heavily and wait ; for in the sun,
Unpitied, scoffed at, cursed at, spit upon,
Hang, maddening in their horrible agony,
Six Mollahs, each impaled upon his stake.

   *   *   *   * .   *   *

· Here is a dell of Evening Primroses,
Which bow their heads, like weeping Magdalens,
Around the cross-foot of a carven Christ
Upon the edge of a wood.   O loveliest flower,
Whose delicate petals, tinctured like yon sky, '
Faint twilight lemon, rival thy sweet breath
In tender salutation of the sense !   .
Fosterer of gentle dreams ! why look'st thou now
Like a soft incarnation of Love's soul,
Like Mercy pleading at the gate of Hell,
Like new-born Pity in the ugly world
Of human misery?   Perhaps when dawned
The day of woman's hope, and women brought
Their children to their Saviour, those blest eyes
Pitied thy faint, sweet blossoms, as they fell
Withering from infant hands.   Perhaps his tears
Were rained upon them ere he knelt by night,
Drinking, for man, the inevitable cup
Of Earth's despair in lone Gethsemane.

THE CHRIST OF THE TITI-SEE.

1.

Poor pale Christ that hang'st there dumbly,
    Spear and sponge thy cross beside,
With thy crown of thorns upon thee,
    And thy blood-streams never dried !

2.

Wherefore comest thou to haunt me,
    With thy wide wounds gaping red ?
All last night thy dolorous vision
    Glared at me beside my bed.

3.

With that look of mute upbraiding
    In thy ghastly face of pain,
Dost thou ask, " Have I, the Saviour,
    Died for this bad world in vain ? "

4.

Eighteen centuries and three-quarters
  Since that world, O Blessed One,
Heard thy death-cry, " It is finished ! "
  Criest Thou now, " Is it begun ? "

A DREAM OF JUDGMENT.

I.

A WEIRD, wild dream this morning,
   I dreamt as in bed I lay,
That One was come to Judgment at last,
   The Christ of the Titi-See !

2.

The terrible Judgment-Trumpet
   Brayed loud as the Righi horn,
And summoned to meet by the Titi-See,
   All folk that ever were born.

3.

Through the chill, grey, last morning
   Pealed on its shuddering tones,
And slowly, drowsily, out of our graves
   We dragged our clattering bones.

4.

In the chill, grey, last morning,
  Half-waked, we shivering stood,
And strove to blanket our bones with flesh
  Hastily, as we could.

5.

In terror, upon his death-bed
  The sun lay, loth to rise ;
Grey Dawn, with her doomsday candle,
  Made ghastly gleam in the skies.

6.

And crowding, struggling, striving,
  We hurried a doleful way
To where, 'mid angels, stood in the sky
  The Christ of the Titi-See.

7.

On either hand an angel
  Stood, holding the sponge and spear,
And in His face the terrible look
  Froze our weak bones with fear.

8.

He spoke not a word of cursing,
  But with each glittering eye,
That shone like a star in his weary face,
  He damned us utterly.

9.

The blood ran down in great rivers,
  From his red wounds ne'er dried;
With bloody fire the Titi-See
  It kindled from side to side;

10.

And struggling, shuddering, and striving,
  Our bones all a-quake for fear,
The angels down to that Lake of Fire
  Drove us with sponge and spear.

11.

I woke: my innocent lakelet
  Was glittering in the sun,
In dewy pastures cows were abroad,
  The beautiful day begun.

12.

Through fields a-shimmer with hairbells
  I took my lonely way,
To where hung bleeding, with piteous face,
  The Christ of the Titi-See.

GOLGOTHA.

1.

On his cross still hangs the Saviour,
  Bears our sins in dreadful sum,
Eighteen centuries and three quarters,
  Yet his kingdom is not come.

2.

"It is finished!"   Was it finished
  When thy path of pain was trod?
Thou didst bear the sins of mortals,
  Who shall bear the sins of God?

THE MODERN GETHSEMANE.

1.

No, I'm no god, alas! Christ or Prometheus—
What boots my anguish? The blood of my passion
Works no redemption. Ah! wearied with sorrow,
Pale and reproachful, ye poor and opprest ones,
With sullen eyes will ye wither my roses,
      Passing me moaning?

2.

Call you these roses? Nay, here be great blood-drops
Blown into flowers—see! If this be a garden,
Name it Gethsemane. Still, ye opprest ones,
With weary eyes will ye pass by my roses?

3.

Is it my fault that my blood brings no healing?
Think ye my anguish the less, being little,
Dull, unheroic; my mountain of passion
This poor, small garden? What look ye to me for?

4.

Come ye for grapes filled with wine of redemption,
Holy, newbirthful, the blood eucharistic
Of a great Lamb slain?   Nay, I'm but a small one—
Sad as your eyes as ye pass by my roses.

5.

Yet, even for me, 'mid the clouds of some dawning,
Pale, like the ghost of Life's babe, tranquil, terrible,
I may see standing the angel of agony,
With new, strange chalice—shall I not drink it?

6.

Ah ! what avails it ?   The blood of my passion,
What can it purchase ? When, six long hours hanging,
Loud, with rent heart, I would cry, " It is finished !"
Were the world saved? I, alas ! am no Saviour.

7.

I would hang twelve, though, for my little world's sake,
I would hang twelve, would my Father in Heaven
Heal but Love's wounds, and I felt through the death-
    swoon
There at my cross-foot the Magdalen standing,
Kissing the blood from my feet, loving, weeping,
    Beautiful, with long hair.

SONG-TIDE.

SONG-TIDE.

1.

SOMETIMES when long, long frozen,
   My heart's all bleak and drear,
Some tiniest thing that grows in
   Its meadows forth will peer.

2.

Out of the frost-bound clay there,
   It peeps, I know not how;
And soon all turns to May there,
   Green buds on every bough.

3.

Then flowers that have slept long time,
   Spring fragrant from the mould,
And then begins my song-time,
   My heart's new Age of Gold.

4.

From far-off countries shyly
  Old songs fly back once more,
And soon new young ones slyly
  Come twittering by the score.

5.

Once lazily I'd watch them
  Fly off and disappear,
But now I fain would catch them
  To sing beside thine ear.

THE DEAD NUPTIAL.

It was a nuptial of the dead,
Hope was a corse when she was wed,
Her loathèd bridegroom was Decay,
And Sorrow gave the bride away;
And the wedding-priest was Care,
And the bride-bed's fruit, Despair.

THE BLACK KNIGHT.

1.

A BEATEN and a baffled man,
  My life drags lamely day by day,
Too young to die, too old to plan,
    In failure grey.

2.

The knights ride east, the knights ride west,
  For ladyes' tokens blithe of cheer,
Each bound upon some gallant quest;
    While I rust here.

SONG.

1.

CHILL November's sullen breath
  Wraps the torpid heavens in cloud,
All the woods lie still in death,
  With the brooding mist for shroud.

2.

Winter now no more in scorn
  Day by day the world reprieves,
And the frail flowers latest born
  Moulder with the mouldering leaves.

3.

All things sink to gloomy rest,
  Cold the fallow sleeps in gloom,
Cold my heart lies in my breast,
  Like a corpse within the tomb.

4.

But when spring bids flower and bird
Wake with joy, in winter's bane,
Then may Love with magic word
Raise my heart to life again.

RECONCILIATION.

1.

Dare not to tell me I have lost thee,
  Thy heart will give thy tongue the lie ;
The hopes thou hast wrecked, the tears I've cost thee,
  Like wailing ghosts against thee cry.

2.

Mine, mine thou art—our spirits mingled
  Eagerly once as fire and air,
Fated for aye to live unsingled,
  Or pine apart in pale despair.

3.

Dare not to tell me thou hast found me
  For thy great dreams too mean a thing ;
Thy faith that saved, thy love that crowned me,
  Will plead for their anointed king.

4.

Kiss me once more !   Thy sin's forgiven ;
   Forgive me mine.   Oh, never more
May we two sulk, so long unshríven,
   While weeping Love holds wide the door !

GHOSTS.

1.

Now the world of day is dead,
And the faces that I dread
Crowd around my sleepless bed,
   From the grey, sepulchral past,
   With some nameless woe aghast—
Faces of the wistful dead.

2.

Pale, companionless, they crowd,
Each, with lonely eyes not proud,
Sewn into his lonely shroud !
   Oh, ye dead, do ye deplore
   On some loveless, Stygian shore,
Love's wan gleam to earth allowed?

3·

Could I learn your wants to know
As I knew them long ago,
Then ye would not fright me so ;
    But your looks are wan and strange,
    As though some Stygian wind of change
Through your withering hearts did blow.

SONG.

1.

As drooping fern for dewdrops,
　For flowers the bee,
Wave-weary birds for woodlands,
　Long I for thee.

2.

As rivers seek the ocean,
　Tired things their nest,
As storm-worn ships their haven,
　Seek I thy breast.

NOCTURNE.

I.

INTO the night, the odorous summer night,
I wander, driven of Love, whose breath of joy
Suffuses all the radiance of the sky
And dimness of the earth like slumber now.

2.

O summer night, O scented summer night !
Where walks my Love—through what deep dells
    of peace ?
Fill her with the rich ache of my desire,
Sandal her feet with speed to come to me.

3.

The golden summer dusk broods in the boughs,
Between the starlight pale and glimmering lake ;
The night's heart throbs, and with it throbs my
    own,
Through the wild-throbbing throat of nightingales.

4.

O summer night, O blissful summer night,
Who feedest with thy love the heavenly flocks,
Kiss my fair Love, and feed her with my life,
Tell her my arms with thine are round her thrown !

AN AUTUMN LOVE SONG.

THE frail flowers are dying,
The thistledown flying,
   Summer is past !
The first leaves that wither
Roam hither and thither
   With the treacherous blast ;
And away to dark ruin he will ravish at last
   Their green mates from the bough,
   Where they sigh and tremble now.

2.

The surges are shattered,
The tough ragweed tattered
   By the gusts of the gale ;

O'er lowland and highland,
And round the green island,
    A wanderer pale,
Strays. the sunshine; the moor seethes with
    whispers of wail,
    As its reed-grasses shake,
    And serely shudders the brake.

3.

The leaves and the surges
May chaunt their wild dirges,
    The pale flowers pine;
My heart at their voices
More hugely rejoices;
    One draught of Love's wine
Unwinters the earth—thou art mine, thou art
    mine!
    Let the wind have its will,
    And rave: I glow in its chill!

4.

Thy kisses, warm-clinging,
My heart have set singing;
    Autumn's at bay!

One rose blooms unmarred in
My yew-cloistered-garden—
I'll pluck it to-day,
And bid it go die in thy bosom, and say
With its passionate breath :
" Love greets thee—victor o'er death ! "

A PHANTASY.

I.

A LITTLE moth, and a star fading in heaven !
  Happy were the days that I spent with thee, Father
    of waters !
Happy were the days in the sumach-grove by the
    sea,
  When thou and I were comrades, Father of waters !

2.

Something beyond a hope from the opening eye of
    the East,
  Something deeper than joy from the bosom of all
    things fair
Came to me then ; and yet I saw in the kindling sky
  Only a little moth, and a star fading from heaven.

SNAKE-CHARM.

1.

INTO this dusky bower
  Of sylvan quiet,
Where roses and rank vines
  Only run riot,
Whence comest thou, dark Shape, at this sweet hour,
  Into this lonely bower?

2.

" I am the spectral form
  Of hopes forgotten,
Birth-strangled babes of joy
  Left to grow rotten,
Corpses of unborn deeds, devoured still warm
  By sloth's corrupting swarm."

3.

Welcome, thou dismal guest,
Sit down beside me,
Lie by me all night long,
Sting me and chide me.
At dawn I'll gather fruits to lull thy rest,
Thou serpent of the breast !

A DIRGE FOR SUMMER.

1.

How the leaves fall !
The reeds and sere sedges
On the river's brown edges,
  Are singing their dirge ;
For, as Hermes drives ghosts,
The wild wind through their hosts
  Careers with his scourge,
    Overmastering them all.
    How fast the leaves fall !

2.

How the days fail !
Here Summer lies dying,
While we dreamed he was flying
  From afar to our shore !

The days that grew longer,
And sunnier, and stronger,
Shall we ne'er see them more?
Must they dwindle and pale?
Ah ! how fast the days fail !

A SONG OF NIGHT AND DEATH.

I.

DAY's delights are manifold,
Crowned with each his crown of gold;
But gentle Night brings silver peace,
And healing sleep, and toil's surcease.
    Kind Night, fold thy wings
    Over all day-weary things!

2.

Life may bring us with full hands
Glorious gifts from happy lands;
But gentle Death, with drowsy kiss,
Gives us rest from bale and bliss.
    Kind Death, on thy breast
    May all life-weary things have rest!

LONGING.

1.

There's tempest in the sky to-night,
  There's longing in my heart—
O couldst thou feel its passionate glow,
  Now, now, where'er thou art !

2.

Lonely I walk the lonely road,
  The sea low moans behind,
O'erhead, through glimmering leaves, my soul
  Sighs with the sighing wind.

3.

Faint balm from ghost-white meadow-sweet,
  Wavering the reeds above,
Breathes to my heart how, wert thou here,
  I best could speak my love.

4.

I'd fold thee from the winds away,
My arms thy blissful nest,
Reverently, sadly, tenderly,
To kiss thy warm, sweet breast.

PARTING.

I.

Oh, keep me in thy heart, love,
　Oh, keep me in thy heart!
For though from thee I part, love,
　Deep, deep in mine thou art.

2.

Both day and night I love thee,
　Love me both night and day,
And day and night above thee
　Hover Love's wings, I pray!

ABSENCE.

1.

DEAREST, where'er thou art,
　　The birds are singing,
I fold thee to my heart
　　With arms close-clinging.

2.

The changes of Love's year
　　Keep hearts a-beating,
Partings that bring more near
　　Make blissful meeting.

THE DREAM.

1.

THERE wakes the Dawn, and from her flies my dream,
　　A dream of feverish thoughts and foolish fears
That filled the ear of Sleep with troublous theme,
　　My heart with anguish, and mine eyes with tears.

2.

I dreamed that we had parted for a day,
　　As now; but envious Death's remorseless door
Was shut between us, and a wall of clay
　　Barred me from sight of thee for evermore.

3.

But night is flown, and morn with amber eyes
　　Looks through the clouds, and with her fly my fears;
Upon thy living sleep the sun will rise—
　　Pure love it is that fills mine eyes with tears.

4.

Oh, not despair this coming morn foretells,
  Death dares not blast my blossom to the core !
My love, that gushes warm from life's deep wells,
  Bids my heart sing, for we shall meet once more.

A MESSAGE.

1.

My heart, a cage-bird pining,
  I bore across the sea;
Now, in glad dawn, soar shining
  Its free wings back to thee.

2.

My kisses, 'twill not lose them
  In flying o'er the foam,
And it will find thy bosom
  Surely as doves their home.

HOMEWARD.

1.

THERE'S sunshine in my heart I trow,
　My own love, my true love;
For homeward, homeward speed I now—
　Feel'st thou my coming too, love?

2.

The way that looked but bleak before,
　My true love, my own love,
Wears blither face than once it wore,
　When I had left thee lone, love.

3.

The flowers I saw not in the night,
　My fair love, my sweet love,
Wave, as I pass their greetings bright,
　I'll give thee when we meet, love.

4.

There's not a thing that hath God's grace,
  My sweet love, my fair love,
But makes me think of thy sweet face,
  And love thee more than e'er, love.

MEETING.

1.

My own love, my true love,
   I hug thee to my heart !
My love springs ever new, love,
   Whether we meet or part.

2.

I love thee, sleeping, waking,
   I love thee, near or far ;
But best when we are slaking
   Love's thirst, as now we are.

SONNETS.

"I could be bounded in a nut-shell, and count myself a king of infinite space."—*Hamlet.*

MAGNOLIAS.

Thou pale sad moon, slow-waning, night by night,
From thy fair throne, when nightly thou didst busk
Thy swelling bosom in more silvery light,
I breathed on Como's shore the odorous dusk
Of great magnolias ! Whiter than the tusk
Of Indian elephant, like beakers bright,
Their Bacchic flowers they lifted in delight, ·
And made libation of their winy musk.
To thee they made libation, and their leaves
Murmured of joy's increase ; yet never more
Shall they nor I renew beneath thy spell
That joy. Thou changest ; and my spirit grieves
That naught may be as it hath been before,
That welcome makes sad music with farewell.

A DAY-DREAM IN KENT.

IN some remote, rich tract of Keats's mind
These woodlands might have grown, where all day
    long
Ten thousand nightingales their moonlight song
Rehearse, with bursting notes that load the wind
Like hyacinth-bells in spring.   Sweet chance to find
In one delicious jungle, green and strong,
Growths of all climes—see birch-stems shine along
Dim rhododendron thickets, overtwined
With English woodbine !   In so fair a dream
Those pigeons might be thoughts, through dream-lit
    glades
Winging their way to shadowy haunts unknown.
For ever might they fly ; for ever gleam
Their wings through happier woods ; each songster
    lone
For ever warble in more bowery shades !

LOVE AND LIFE.

I MET Love wandering in the fields of Life,
Whose arrows, winged with joy and barbed with pain,
Had marred his fair Olympian limbs,—in vain,
For with his dreaming eyes, blind to all strife,
He held his way, and, often left for slain,
Still rose, to spend his shafts on things despised,
Weak, sad, uncomely things ; and I, surprised
To see him idiot-like, such mien maintain,
Questioned him as he passed why this was so.
Then, for all answer, with a martyr's smile,
He bent his golden bow, and all my heart
In sudden flame I found, and grew to know
Strange secrets of the melancholy Isle,
Where Life and Love, the twins, were torn apart.

A DREAM OF EGYPT.

" Where's my Serpent of old Nile ? "

NIGHT sends forth many an eagle-wingèd dream
To soar through regions never known by day;
And I by one of these was rapt away
To where the sun-burnt Nile, with opulent stream
Makes teem the desert sand.   My pomp supreme
Enriched the noon;   I spurned earth's common
     clay;
For I was Antony, and by me lay
That Snake whose sting was bliss.   Nations did
     seem
But camels for the burden of our joy;
Kings were our slaves; our wishes glowed in the
     air
And grew fruition; night grew day, day night,
Lest the high bacchanal of our loves should cloy;
We reined the tiger, Life, with flower-crowned hair,
Abashlessly abandoned to delight.

TO THE ALBANI ATHENA.

WHAT was he, man or more, whose valorous brain
Endured anew the throes of Zeus, and wrought
Glad self-deliverance when this virgin thought
Leaped forth full-armed to ease creation's pain?
Waste is that womb of gods; thou dost remain
Orphaned, alone.   So stood grave Pallas, fraught
With radiant power, and gazed her foes to naught,
Calm sentinel of her Athenian fane !
August, serene, austere, thou marble dream
Of her, the holiest life of living Greece,
Terrible Maid ! did thy creator bow
In a sublime abasement, when the beam
Of thy full beauty awed his hand to cease—
Transfigured by stern love—as I do now?

A JULY NIGHT.

THE dreamy, long, delicious afternoon
That filled the flowers with honey, and made well
With earliest nectar many a secret cell
Of pulping peaches, with a murmurous tune
Lulled all the woods and leas ; but now, how soon
The winds have woke to break the sultry spell—
The drowsy flocks, that low in the west did dwell,
Like Oreads chased fleet madly by the moon !
So, Cleopatra-like, has rich July,
A Queen of many moods, outdreamed the day
To hold by night wild revel.   Odours warm
Come panted with each gust, as royally,
Magnificent alike in calm or storm,
With some voluptuous anger she would play.

THE MARSEILLAISE.

WHAT means this mighty chant, wherein the wail
Of some intolerable woe, grown strong
With sense of more intolerable wrong,
Swells to a stern victorious march—a gale
Of vengeful wrath? What mean the faces pale,
The fierce resolve, the ecstatic pangs along
Life's fiery ways, the demon thoughts which throng
The gates of awe, when these wild notes assail
The sleeping of our souls? Hear ye no more
Than the mad foam of revolution's leaven,
Than a roused people's throne-o'erwhelming tread?
Hark! 'tis man's spirit thundering on the shore
Of iron fate; the tramp of titans dread,
Sworn to dethrone the gods unjust from heaven.

PRINTED BY WILLIAM CLOWES AND SONS, LIMITED, LONDON AND BECCLES.

www.ingramcontent.com/pod-product-compliance
Lightning Source LLC
Chambersburg PA
CBHW020759020726
47495CB00008B/2503